ORY
OL
STARS

Don't Break the Balance Beam!

by Jessica Gunderson
illustrated by Jorge Santillan

STONE ARCH BOOKS
a capstone imprint

VICTORY SCHOOL SUPERSTARS

Sports Illustrated KIDS *Don't Break the Balance Beam!*
is published by Stone Arch Books — A Capstone Imprint
151 Good Counsel Drive, P.O. Box 669
Mankato, Minnesota 56002
www.capstonepub.com

Art Director and Designer: Bob Lentz
Creative Director: Heather Kindseth
Production Specialist: Michelle Biedscheid

Timeline photo credits: Shutterstock/Valenta (top left);
Sports Illustrated/Andy Hayt (middle left), Manny Millan
(bottom right), Tony Triolo (top right).

Library of Congress Cataloging-in-Publication Data is
available on the Library of Congress website.

ISBN: 978-1-4342-2057-8 (library binding)
ISBN: 978-1-4342-2807-9 (paperback)

Summary: Kenzie is scared to perform on the balance beam
after her super strength causes her to break a beam.

Printed in the United States of America in Stevens Point, Wisconsin.
032010   005741WZF10

TABLE of CONTENTS

KENZIE WINZ

AGE: 10 SPORT: Gymnastics
SUPER SPORTS ABILITY: Super strength makes this tumbler soar.

VICTORY SCHOOL SUPERSTARS

KENZIE

CARMEN

DANNY

KENZIE

JOSH

ALICIA

TYLER

Super Strength

"It's your turn, Kenzie!" calls Coach Trish.

I take a deep breath and stare at the balance beam in front of me. I hear giggling behind me. It's my teammate Wendy.

"Are you scared?" she asks with a little laugh.

I glare at her. Wendy is never scared. Wendy can do everything.

"I'm not scared," I growl.

Coach Trish smiles at me. "Come on, Kenzie. The tryouts for the advanced team are tomorrow. You have to practice the beam."

I know I shouldn't be scared of the balance beam, especially here, at the Victory School for Super Athletes.

Victory is a place for kids who are gifted in sports. All the students have special abilities that make them stronger and faster than normal kids. We are known as the Victory Superstars.

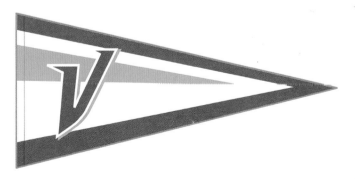

My ability is super strength. How does super strength help me in gymnastics? When I do flips, handsprings, and cartwheels, I can fly at least twenty feet into the air. It's all that leg power!

But up on that beam, I forget about my abilities. I'm a pile of nerves.

I take another deep breath. I try to block out Wendy and the other kids who are watching me.

I look toward the springboard at one end of the balance beam. I will do an easy mount onto the balance beam. I'll jump off the springboard and land with both feet on the beam.

I start running, but when I reach the springboard, I just stop. I can't do it. My heart is beating so hard it might burst. My heartbeat is the only sound in the entire gym.

I just can't do it. I'll never be able to work the balance beam again. Not after what happened last week.

Control Your Strength

I used to be good at the balance beam. Not as good as Wendy, of course. No one is as good as Wendy. Wendy's special skill is flexibility. She can twist her body into a pretzel and still stay on the beam. No wonder everyone calls her Bendy Wendy.

My special strength can be a problem on the beam. Coach Trish is always telling me, "You have to learn to control your strength."

When I don't control it, I push too hard. There is too much power, and I lose my balance. And then I fall. Falling can be embarrassing, but nothing compares to what happened last week.

Last week, the parents of all the Victory Superstars came to watch the gymnastics team. The gym was crowded with people.

Soon it was my turn on the balance beam. I mounted the beam with no problems. Then I went into the forward splits. I lifted myself up with my arms. Back walkovers across the beam were next. I heard Coach Trish's words in my head: "Control your strength."

But the cheers were so loud, and I felt so excited. I pushed off hard from the beam into the back handspring. I forgot all about controlling my strength. My hands came down on the beam just as hard as I'd pushed off.

And then it happened. I broke the balance beam right in two.

The crowd's cheers turned into gasps. I'm sure that was the first time they had seen that happen. The worst part was hearing my teammates laughing.

The mats below the beam kept me from getting hurt, at least on the outside. Inside, I felt terrible. I didn't talk to anyone. I just ran out of the gym. I knew I would never be able to do the balance beam again.

Beam Breaker

I can't look at the balance beam without remembering the break. I can still hear the cracking sound. And I can still hear my teammates' laughter. Some of the girls have even started calling me "B.B." It's short for "Beam Breaker." I hate it!

But now I have to get my focus back on practice. Coach Trish crosses her arms and looks down at me.

"Go practice your balance routine on the floor," she says. "And remember, control your strength."

I walk over to the floor mats, feeling terrible. Why can't I just get back on the beam? I have to try again.

Suddenly I hear clapping. I turn just in time to see Wendy leap onto the beam. She cartwheels into the splits. Then Wendy raises herself into a handstand. The whole thing is perfect.

"You'll win a gold medal one day, Bendy Wendy!" someone yells.

"I hope so!" Wendy yells back. It isn't fair. Everything comes so easy to her.

I turn back to the mats. There is a line of tape on the floor in front of me. It is the same length and width as the balance beam. I perform my routine on the tape. Two cartwheels, the splits, and a back handspring. I don't push too hard or lose my balance. My routine is perfect.

But nobody notices.

Fear of Falling

I do my routine on the floor a few more times before practice is over. As I go to gather my things, I hear someone clapping behind me. It's my good friend Alicia.

"Hey, Alicia," I say. Alicia, with her super jumping ability, is a cheerleader at Victory.

"Your routine looks great," she says.

"Sure, as long as I can do it on the floor," I say. "I'm afraid to go back on the beam."

"Come on. You can't let what happened freak you out," Alicia tells me.

"Are you kidding? Have you ever broken a balance beam in front of hundreds of people?" I ask.

"No, but remember that pep rally when I jumped too close to the basketball hoop? I ended up stuck in the net. Talk about embarrassing!" she says.

"That was actually pretty funny!" I say. She shoots me a dirty look.

"Come on," I add. "You have to admit that it was."

"Maybe," she says with a grin. "I'm glad it cheered you up. The point is I didn't let it stop me. That night I still went out there and cheered. I even performed the same routine I messed up on."

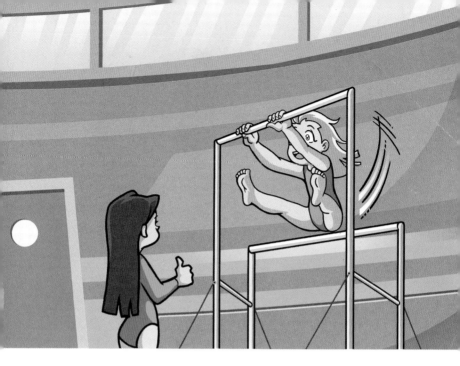

"I know I have to try again. I just get so nervous. I wish I could just do my floor routine," I say.

"Well, you are a great tumbler. You were the first girl in our class to do a perfect back handspring," says Alicia with a smile.

I smile too. I *was* the first. Even before Wendy.

Then my smile fades. "I have to make my routine perfect by tomorrow's team tryouts," I say. "And after that, I never want to do the beam again!"

Alicia gives me a funny look. "I know that gymnasts have special events. But don't you have to compete in more than one area?"

"Yeah, I guess. At least on the advanced team," I admit.

"Well, then there is just one thing to do," says Alicia.

"What?" I ask.

"Get back on that beam. Don't worry. What are the chances you would break two beams in one week?" Alicia teases.

I'm not ready to laugh about it, but I know she is right.

Just then Coach Trish walks up to us. "I couldn't help but overhear. Alicia is right, you know," she tells me. "Are you ready to try the beam?"

I nod, walk over to the beam, and jump up onto it. "Control your strength," I say to myself as I push into a back handspring.

Whoosh! I push too hard. I'm not going to break the beam, but I am going to miss my landing. Before I know it, I'm laying flat on the mat below.

Coach Trish shakes her head. "Kenzie, you must have confidence. You must believe you can do it."

I look over at Wendy, who is putting chalk on her hands. Wendy smiles and waves, then she jumps up on the beam.

"Wendy makes the beam look so easy,"
I say.

"That's what a good gymnast does,"
Coach Trish says.

The Tryouts

The next day, I wake up feeling nervous and excited. I know I can do my balance beam routine. I just need confidence and control.

At school, the gym is packed with parents and students who have come to watch the tryouts.

I spot my parents and Alicia and wave. Wendy starts stretching next to me. I watch as her arms fold behind her back. How can anyone be so flexible?

"Don't be nervous, Kenzie," Wendy says. "I know you'll make the team."

"I don't know . . ." I say.

"I'm nervous, too," Wendy admits. "About tumbling."

"But tumbling is easy," I say.

"It is for you," Wendy says. "You have super strength. You can fly through the air like a cannonball! I'll never be as good as you in tumbling."

I smile at Wendy. I guess Wendy isn't as perfect as I always thought she was.

I wait and watch as others take their turns on the beam. I can't help feeling nervous. Coach Trish notices the worried look on my face.

"Remember . . ." she begins.

"Control my strength," I finish.

I'm up. I mount the beam and take a deep breath. This time, I won't think about breaking the balance beam. I won't even think about falling.

I balance on one foot for a few seconds. Then I turn on my toes and lean into a cartwheel. Eyes up. Don't look down. I feel one foot touch the beam, and then the other. I didn't fall!

I feel sure of myself as I complete another cartwheel. But the hardest part is still to come, the back handspring. I need just the right amount of strength. Not too much and not too little.

I see Coach Trish and Wendy out of the corner of my eye. Wendy gives me a thumbs-up sign.

I breathe in and focus on my balance. Then I push off from my feet into the handspring. My hands touch the beam. I spring from my hands.

Have I pushed too hard? I wonder.

A split-second later, my feet land on the beam. I wobble just a little, but I don't fall. And the balance beam doesn't break.

No one is laughing at me this time. Today, there is nothing but cheers.

I finish my routine and look at Coach Trish, who is grinning. The tryouts aren't over yet, but I can tell that I made the team.

Teammates

I run toward the edge of the gym to prepare for my next event, tumbling. Now that I nailed the beam, I am ready to really cut loose on the floor. I can't wait.

"You did it!" I hear Alicia's voice squealing behind me. She leaps over to me and gives me a big hug. "I always knew you could do it," she says.

I hug Alicia back. "Thanks for believing in me," I say.

I notice Wendy sticking her landing off the beam. Even though I missed her routine, I know it was perfect.

Wendy walks toward us, her arms open. She hugs me tightly.

"Your beam routine was awesome!" Wendy exclaims. "I just know that we will both make the advanced team."

"For sure," I say with a grin. "Bendy Wendy and B.B. will make great teammates!"

SUPERSTAR OF THE WEEK
Kenzie Winz

Kenzie Winz's super strength caused her big problems on the balance beam. But she learned to control her strength and overcome her fears. For that, we are making her our Superstar of the Week.

Kenzie, your super strength was a problem on the beam. Has it ever caused you trouble before?
Oh, sure! Like in kindergarten, we went to the zoo for a field trip. I snuck in and picked up one of the elephants. Boy, was my teacher mad! The zookeeper was mad, too!

How old were you when you started gymnastics?
I was four. I didn't like it at first, but then I got hooked.

Were you good right away?
No! People sometimes think that, but I had a lot to learn. I couldn't even do a cartwheel until I was five.

What is your favorite subject in school?
I like reading. I love books!

And what about your favorite treat?
Um . . . that is hard. Either brownies or ice cream. Maybe both! Brownies with ice cream on top.

GLOSSARY

abilities (uh-BIL-i-teez)—skills or powers

back walkovers (BAK WAWK-oh-vurs)—stunts in which you go from a standing position back to a bridge, then kick back to a standing position

balance beam (BAL-uhnss BEEM)—a narrow beam used in gymnastics, usually about four feet off the floor

confidence (KON-fuh-dehns)—a feeling of certainty

embarrassing (em-BA-ruhss-ing)—something that makes you feel awkward and uncomfortable

flexibility (flek-suh-BIL-uh-tee)—the ability to bend

gasps (GASPS)—sudden breaths

handsprings (HAND-springs)—stunts in which you spring forward or backward onto both hands, then flip all the way over to land on your feet

routine (roo-TEEN)—a set of moves a gymnast performs

springboard (SPRING-bord)—a springy board that helps a gymnast jump high into the air

tumbler (TUHM-blur)—someone who does cartwheels, handsprings, and other gymnastic moves

GYMNASTICS IN HISTORY

2500 B.C. A **live bull** is used in a gymnastics event in ancient Greece.

1811 A.D. The first gymnastics center opens near Berlin, Germany.

1928 Women gymnasts compete in the Olympics for the first time.

1970 Cathy Rigby wins a silver medal at the world championships. She is the first American to win a world medal in gymnastics.

1976 **Nadia Comaneci** from Romania scores the first perfect 10 in Olympic history.

1984 American **Mary Lou Retton** wins top all-around gymnast at the Olympics. *Sports Illustrated* names her Sportswoman of the Year.

1996 The **U.S. women's team** wins the team gold medal at the Olympics. They are nicknamed the "Magnificent Seven."

2006 Gymnastic scoring is changed. Gymnasts can no longer earn a **perfect 10**. Some gymnasts and coaches do not like the new system.

2010 China's Winter Olympics snowboarding team includes former gymnasts.

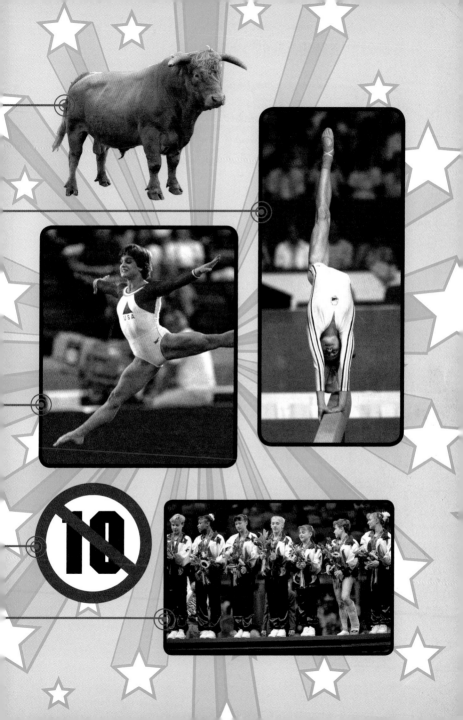

VICTORY ★ SCHOOL SUPERSTARS

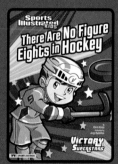
Read them ALL!